Spawn of tl

H. Thompson Rich

Alpha Editions

This edition published in 2024

ISBN : 9789361471445

Design and Setting By
Alpha Editions
www.alphaedis.com
Email - info@alphaedis.com

As per information held with us this book is in Public Domain.
This book is a reproduction of an important historical work. Alpha Editions uses the best technology to reproduce historical work in the same manner it was first published to preserve its original nature. Any marks or number seen are left intentionally to preserve its true form.

Spawn of the Comet

By H. Thompson Rich

>Tokyo, June 10 (AP).—A number of the meteors that pelted Japan last night, as the earth passed through the tail of the Mystery Comet have been found and are puzzling astronomers everywhere.
>
>About the size of baseballs, orange in color, they appear to be of some unknown metal. So far, due to their extreme hardness, all attempts to analyze them have failed.
>
>Their uniformity of size and marking gives rise to the popular belief that they are seeds, and, fantastic though this conception is, it finds support in certain scientific quarters here.

JIM CARTER read the news dispatch thoughtfully and handed it back to his chief without comment.

"Well, what do you make of it?"

Miles Overton, city editor of *The New York Press*, shoved his green eye-shade far back on his bald head and glanced up irritably from his littered desk.

"I don't know," said Jim.

"You don't know!" Overton snorted, biting his dead cigar impatiently. "And I suppose you don't know they're finding the damn things right here in New York, not to mention Chicago, London, Rio and a few other places," he added.

"Yes, I know about New York. It's a regular egg hunt."

"Egg hunt is right! But why tell me all this now? I didn't see any mention of 'em in your report of last night's proceedings. Did you see any?"

"No, but I saw a lot of shooting stars!" said Jim, recalling that weird experience he and the rest of humanity had passed through so recently.

"Yeah, I'll say!" Overton lit his wrecked cigar and dragged on it soothingly. "Now then, getting back to cases—what are these damn things, anyway? That's what I'd like to know."

"So would I," said Jim. "Maybe they *are* seeds?"

Overton frowned. He was a solid man, not given to fancies. He had a paper to get out every day and that taxed his imagination to the limit. There was no gray matter left for any such idle musings as Jim suggested. What he wanted was facts, and he wanted them right away.

"Eggs will do!" he said. "Go out and get one—and find out what's inside it."

"Okay, Chief," said Jim, but he knew it was a large order. "I'll have one on your desk for breakfast!"

Then, with a grave face that denied his light words, he stepped from the city room on that fantastic assignment.

IT was the television broadcast hour and crowds thronged the upper level of Radio Plaza, gazing, intently at the bulletin screen, as Jim Carter emerged from the Press tower.

News from the ends of the earth, in audio-picture form, flashed before their view; but only the reports on the strange meteors from the tail of 1947, IV—so designated by astronomers because it was the fourth comet discovered that year—held their interest. Nothing since the great Antarctic gold rush of '33 had so gripped the public as the dramatic arrival and startling behavior of this mysterious visitant from outer space.

Jim paused a moment, halfway across the Plaza, to take a look at the screen himself.

The substance of the Tokyo dispatch, supplemented by pictures of Japanese scientists working over the baffling orange spheres, had just gone off. Now came a flash from Berlin, in which a celebrated German chemist was seen directing an effort to cut into one of them with an acid drill. It failed and the scientist turned to declare to the world that the substance seemed more like crystal than metal and was harder than diamond.

Jim tarried no longer. He knew where he was going. It was still early and Joan would be up—Joan Wentworth, daughter of Professor Stephen Wentworth, who held the chair of astro-lithology at Hartford University. It was as their guest at the observatory last night that he had seen 1947, IV at close range, as the earth passed through her golden train with that awesome, unparalleled display of fireworks.

Now he'd have the pleasure of seeing Joan again, and at the same time get the low-down from her father on those confounded seeds—or eggs, rather. If anyone could crack one of them, he'd bet Professor Wentworth could.

So, hastening toward the base of Plaza Airport, he took an elevator to ramp-level 118, where his auto-plane was parked, and five minutes later was winging his way to Hartford.

THROTTLE wide, Jim did the eighty miles to the Connecticut capital in a quarter of an hour.

Then, banking down through the warm June night onto the University landing field, he retracted the wings of his swift little bus and motored to the foot of Observatory Hill.

Parking outside the Wentworth home, he mounted the steps and rang the bell.

It was answered by a slim, appealing girl of perhaps twenty-two. Hers was a wistful, oval face, with a small, upturned nose; and her clear hazel eyes were the sort that always seem to be enjoying some amusing secret of their own. Her hair was a soft brown, worn loose to the shoulders, after the style then in vogue.

"Joan!" blurted Jim.

"What brings you here at such an hour, Jimmy Carter?" she asked with mock severity.

"You!"

"I don't believe you."

"What then have I come for?"

"You've come to interview father about those meteorites."

"Nonsense! That's purely incidental—a mere by-product, you might say."

"Yes, you might—but I wouldn't advise you to say it to father."

"All right, I won't," he promised, as she led him into the library.

Professor Wentworth rose as they entered and laid aside some scientific book he had been reading.

A man of medium height and build, he had the same twinkling hazel eyes as his daughter, though somewhat dimmed from peering at too many stars for too many years.

"Good evening, Jim," he said. "I've rather been expecting you. What is on your mind?"

"Seeds! Eggs! Baseballs!" was the reply, "I don't know what. You've seen the latest television reports, I suppose?" said Jim, noting that the panel on the receiving cabinet across the room was still lit.

"I've seen some of them. Joan has been keeping an eye on the screen mostly, however, while I refreshed my mind on the known chemistry of meteorites. You see, I have a few of those eggs myself, up at the observatory."

"You have?" cried Jim.

He was certainly on the right track!

"Yes. One of my assistants brought them in this afternoon. Would you like to see them?"

"I'll say I would!"

"I rather thought you might," the professor smiled. "Come along, then."

And as Jim turned, he shot a look at Joan, and added:

"You may come too, my dear, if you want."

THEY went out and up the hill to where the great white dome glistened under the stars, and once inside, Jim Carter of *The New York Press* was privileged to see two of those strange objects that had turned the world topsy-turvy.

As the Tokyo dispatch and the Berlin television flash had indicated, they were orange in color, about the size of baseballs.

"Weird looking eggs, all right!" said Jim. "What are they made of, anyway?"

"Some element unknown on earth," replied Professor Wentworth.

"But I thought there were only ninety-two elements in the universe and we'd discovered them all."

"So we have. But don't forget this. We are still trying to split the atom, which nature has done many times and will doubtless do many times again. It is merely a matter of altering the valence of the atoms in an old element; whereupon it shifts its position in the periodic scale and becomes a new element. Nature accomplishes this alchemy by means of great heat, which is certainly to be found in a meteor."

"Particularly when it hits the earth's atmosphere!"

"Yes. And now then, I'd like to have you examine more closely this pair I have here."

Jim lifted one and noted its peculiar smoothness, its remarkable weight for its size; he noted, too, that it was veined with concentric markings, like a series of arabesques or fleurs-de-lis.

The professor lifted the other, calling attention to the fact that the size and marking of both were identical, as hitherto reported.

"Also, you'll observe that they are slightly warm. In fact, they are appreciably warmer than when they were first brought in. Curious behavior, this, for new-laid cometary eggs! More like seeds germinating than meteorites cooling, wouldn't you say?"

"But good Lord!" Jim was somewhat taken aback to hear this celebrated scientist apparently commit himself to that wild view. "You don't really think they're seeds, do you?"

"Why not?"

"But surely no seeds could survive the temperature they hit getting here."

"No seeds such as we know, true. But what, after all, do we know of the types of life to be found on other planets?"

"Nothing, of course. Only these didn't come from a planet. They came from a comet."

"And who can say a comet is not a disintegrated planet? Or suppose we take the other theory, that it is an eruption from some sun, ours or another. In any event, who can say no life can survive intense heat? Certainly these seeds—or call them meteorites, if you choose—came through the ordeal curiously unscathed."

"Yes, that's true. Funny, too!"

"And another thing is true, Jim. If by chance they *should* be seeds, and *should* germinate, the life they would produce would be something quite alien to our experience, possibly quite inimical to—"

Professor Wentworth broke off abruptly as a startled cry came from Joan, and, turning, they saw her standing with eyes fixed in fascinated horror on the laboratory table.

FOLLOWING her gaze, Jim saw something that caused his own eyes to bulge. The color of those mysterious orange spheres had suddenly, ominously heightened. They lay glowing there like balls of fire.

"Good God!" he gasped. "Look, Professor! Do you see that?"

Professor Wentworth did not answer but himself stood gazing spellbound at the astounding scene.

Even as they looked, the metal table smoldered under the fiery meteorites and melted, and in a little while the meteorites themselves sizzled from view. Flames licked up from the floor; dense, suffocating fumes rose and swirled through the laboratory.

"Quick!" cried Jim, seizing Joan's arm. "Come on, Professor! Never mind trying to save anything. Let's get out of here!"

They staggered from the laboratory and once outside, plunged down the hill. It was none too soon.

Behind them, as they fled, came suddenly two deafening explosions. Looking back, they saw the roof of the observatory tilt crazily; saw the whole building shatter, and erupt like a volcano.

But that, startling though it was, was not all they saw. For now, as they stood there speechless, two incredible forms rose phoenix-like from the flames—two weird monsters, orange against the red, hideous, nightmarish. They saw them hover a moment above that fiery hell, then rise on batlike wings to swoop off into the night.

Nor was that all. As the awed trio stood there halfway down Observatory Hill, following the flight of that pair of demons, other explosions reached their ears, and, turning to the city below, they saw vivid jets of red leap up here and there, saw other orange wings against the night.

While off across the southeast sky, receding fast, spread the Mystery Comet whose tail had sowed the seeds of this strange life.

STILL silent, the trio stood gazing upon that appalling scene for some minutes, while the ruddy shadows of the flaming observatory lit their tense faces.

"Well, the seeds have hatched," said Professor Wentworth at length, in a strained voice. "I am afraid some of the curious who have been gathering those meteorites so eagerly have paid a dear price for them."

"Yes, I'm afraid so," echoed Jim. "We were lucky. If Joan hadn't happened to spot those things just when she did—" He broke off and pressed her hand fondly. "But somehow I can't believe it, even yet. What do you think the things are, Professor?"

"God knows! As I told you, those seeds, should they germinate, would produce something quite alien to our experience; and as I feared, it is a form of life that will not blend well with humanity."

Jim shuddered.

"But look, father!" exclaimed Joan. "They're flying away! They seem to be way up among the stars. Maybe they've left the earth altogether."

Professor Wentworth following his daughter's gaze, saw that many of the monsters were now mere orange pinpoints against the night.

"Let us hope so!" he said fervently.

But in his heart there was no conviction, nor in Jim's, strangely.

ON the way back to New York, Jim had plenty to heighten his uneasiness. The scene below him everywhere was red with conflagrations, the sky everywhere orange with the wings of those fiery moths.

More than one swept perilously close, as he pushed his auto-plane on at top speed; but they showed no inclination to attack, for which he was devoutly thankful.

Over the metropolitan area, the scene was one beggaring description. All the five boroughs were a blazing checker-board. New Jersey, Connecticut, Westchester—all were raging. Hundreds of those deadly bombs must have burst in Manhattan alone.

But the fire department there seemed to have the situation in hand, he noticed as he swept down onto the Plaza landing platform.

Leaving his plane with an attendant, he took the first elevator to the street level, and crossing hastily to the Press tower, mounted to the city room.

There absolute pandemonium raged. Typewriters were sputtering, telegraph keys clicking, phones buzzing, reporters coming and going in a steady stream, mingled with the frantic orders of editors, sub-editors, copy readers, composing-room men and others.

Carter fought through the bedlam to the city editor's desk.

"Sorry I couldn't bring you that egg, Chief," he said, with a grim smile. "I had one right in my hand, but it hatched out on me."

Overton looked up wearily. He was a man who had seen a miracle, a godless miracle that restored his faith in the devil.

"Don't talk—just write!" he growled. "I've seen and heard too much to-night. We're all going to hell, I guess—unless we're already there."

But Jim wasn't ready to write yet.

"What's the dope elsewhere? The same?"

"All over the map! We're frying, from coast to coast."

"And abroad?"

"Cooked, everywhere!" He paused, and turned an imploring face to Jim. "Tell me, Carter—what's happening? You've seen Wentworth, I suppose. What's he make of it?"

"He—doesn't know."

"God help us! Well, go write your story. If we've got a plant by press time, we'll have something on page one to-morrow—if there's anyone to read it."

BY morning the fires in the metropolitan area had been brought under control and it was found that neither the loss of life nor the damage was as great as had at first been feared. Mainly it was the older types of buildings that had suffered the most.

The same thing was true in other parts of the country and elsewhere in the world; and elsewhere, as in New York, people pulled themselves together, cleared up the debris, and went ahead with their occupations. Business was resumed, and rebuilding operations were begun.

Meanwhile, where were those fiery moths that had sprung so devastatingly from their strange cocoons?

For a while no one knew and it was believed they had indeed winged off into interstellar space, as Joan had suggested that night on Observatory Hill.

Then came rumors that damped these hopes, followed by eye-witness reports that altogether dashed them. The bat-like monsters had flown, not off into space, but to the world's waste-lands.

Strange, it was, the instinct that had led them unerringly to the remotest point of each continent. In North America it was the great Arizona desert, in South America the pampas of Argentina, in Europe the steppes of Russia, in Asia the Desert of Gobi, in Africa the Sahara, in Australia the

Victoria; while in the British Isles, Philippines, New Zealand, Madagascar, Iceland, the East Indies, West Indies, South Seas and other islands of the world, the interiors were taken over by the demons, the populace fleeing for their lives.

As for the oceans, no one knew exactly what had happened there, though it was obvious they, too, had received their share of the bombardment on that fateful night; but, while temperatures were found to be somewhat above normal, scientists were of the opinion that the deadly spawn that had fallen there had failed to incubate.

IMMEDIATELY the presence of the monsters in the Arizona desert was verified, Overton called Jim Carter to his desk.

"Well, I've got a big assignment for you, boy," he said, rather more gently than was his fashion. "Maybe you know what, huh?"

"You want me to buzz out and interview those birds?"

"You guessed it. And photograph 'em!"

"Okay, Chief," said Carter, though he knew this would be the toughest job yet.

Overton knew it, too.

"It won't be easy," he said. "And it may be dangerous. You don't have to take the assignment unless you want."

"But I want."

"Good! I thought you would." He regarded the younger man admiringly, almost enviously. "Now, about those photos. The Television News people haven't been able to get a thing, nor the War Department—not so much as a still. So those photos will be valuable."

Overton paused, to let that sink in.

"They'll be worth a million, in fact, in addition to what the War Department offers. And to you they'll be worth ten thousand dollars."

"How come?"

"Because that's what the Old Man said."

"Well, I can use it!" said Jim, thinking of Joan.

"All right. Then go to it!"

LEAVING New York late that night, Carter timed his flight to arrive over the eastern edge of the desert just before dawn.

The trip was uneventful till he crossed the Rockies over New Mexico and eased down into Arizona. Then, flying low and fast, he suddenly caught a glow of color off ahead.

For an instant Jim thought it was the dawn, then called himself a fool. For one thing, the glow was in the west, not the east. And for another, altogether more significant, it was orange.

His quarry!

Pulling his stick back hard, he shot like a rocket to ten thousand feet, figuring that a higher altitude, besides giving him a better view of the lay of the land, would be considerably safer.

Winging on now at that height, he saw the orange tide rise higher in the west by seconds, as he rushed toward God knew what eery lair. He suddenly gasped in amazement, as he saw now something so incredible it left him numb.

Below, looming above the on-rushing horizon was a city! But such a city as the brain of man could scarcely conceive, much less execute—a city of some fluorescent orange material, rising tier on tier, level on level, spreading out over the sandy floor of the desert for miles.

And, as Jim draw nearer, he saw, too, that this weird city was teeming with life—terrible life! Thousands of those hideous monsters were working there like an army of ants in a sand-hill—a sand-hill of glistening, molten glass, it seemed from the air.

Were they building their city from the sand of the desert, these hellish glaciers?

Carter decided to find out.

"Well, here goes!" he muttered, diving straight for that dazzling citadel, one hand on the stick, the other gripping the trigger of his automatic camera. "This'll make a picture for the Old Man, all right!"

Off to the east the dawn was breaking, and he saw, as he swept down, its pearly pastel shades blending weirdly with that blinding orange glare.

Pressing the trigger now, he drove his screaming plane on with throttle wide—and yes, it was glass!—glass of some sort, that crazy nightmare down there.

"Whew!" gasped Carter as waves of dazing heat rose about him. "Boy, but it's hot! I can't stand much of this. Better get out while the getting's good."

But he clenched his teeth, and dove on down to see what those fiery demons looked like. Funny they didn't make any effort to attack. Surely they must see him now.

"Take that, my beauties!—and that!" he gasped, pressing the trigger of his camera furiously.

Then, at a scant two thousand feet, he levelled off, his wings blistering with the heat, and zoomed up again—when to his horror, his engine faltered; died.

IN that agonizing moment it came to Jim that this perhaps was why neither the Television News nor the War Department pilots had been able to get pictures of the hell below.

Had something about that daring heat killed their motors, too, as it had his? Had they plunged like fluttering, sizzling moths into that inferno of orange flame?

"Well, I guess it's curtains!" he muttered.

A glance at his altimeter showed a scant eighteen hundred now. Another glance showed the western boundary of the city, agonizing miles ahead. Could he make it? He'd try, anyway!

So, nursing his plane along in a shallow glide, Jim slipped down through that dazing heat.

"Got to keep her speed up!" he told himself, half deliriously, as he steadily lost altitude. "Can't pancake here, or I'll be a flapjack!"

At an altitude of less than a thousand he levelled off again, eased on down, fully expecting to feel his plane burst into flames. But though his eyebrows crisped and the gas must have boiled, the sturdy little plane made it.

On a long last glide, he put her wheels down on the sandy desert floor, a bare half mile beyond that searing hell.

The heat was still terrific but endurable now. He dared breathe deeper; he found his head clearing. But what was the good of it? It was only a respite. The monsters had seen him, all right—no doubt about that! Already they were swooping out of their weird citadel like a pack of furious hornets.

On they came, incredibly fast, moving in a wide half-circle that obviously was planned to envelop him.

Tense with horror, like a doomed man at the stake, Jim watched the flaming phalanx advance. And now he saw what they really were; saw that his first, fantastic guess had been right.

They were *ants*—or at least more like ants than anything on earth—great fiery termites ten feet long, hideous mandibles snapping like steel, hot from the forge, their huge compound eyes burning like greenish electric fire in their livid orange sockets.

And another thing Jim saw, something that explained why the fearful insects had not flown up to attack him in the air. Their wings were gone!

They had molted, were earthbound now.

THERE was much food for thought in this, but no time to think. Already the creatures were almost on him.

Jim turned his gaze from them and bent over his dials in a last frantic effort to get his motor started. The instinct of self-preservation was dominant now—and to his joy, suddenly the powerful little engine began to hum with life.

He drew one deep breath of infinite relief, then gave her the gun and whirled off down the desert floor, the enraged horde after him.

For agonizing instants it was a nip-and-tuck race. Then as he felt his wheels lift, he pulled hard back on his stick, and swept up and away from the deadly claws that clutched after him in vain.

Climbing swiftly, Jim banked once, swept back, put the bead full on that scattering half-circle of fiery termites, and pressed the trigger of his automatic camera.

"There, babies!" he laughed grimly. "You're in the Rogues' Gallery now!"

Then, swinging off to the northeast, he continued to climb, giving that weird ant-hill a wide berth.

Funny, about those things losing their wings, he was thinking now. Would they grow them again, or were they on the ground for good? And what was their game out there in the desert, anyway?

Questions Jim couldn't answer, of course. Only time would tell. Meanwhile, he had some pictures that would make the Old Man sit up and take notice, not to mention the War Department.

"They'd better get the Army on the job before those babies get air-minded again!" he told himself, as he winged on into the rising sun. "Otherwise the show they've already staged may be only a little curtain-raiser."

JIM'S arrival in the city room of *The New York Press* that afternoon was a triumphant one, for he had radio-phoned the story ahead and extras were out all over the metropolitan area, with relays flashing from the front pages of papers everywhere.

No sooner had he turned over his precious pictures to the photographic department for development than Overton rushed him to a microphone, and made him repeat his experience for the television screen.

But the city editor's enthusiasm died when the negatives came out of the developer.

"There are your pictures!" he said, handing over a bunch of them.

Carter looked at them in dismay. They were all blank—just so much plain black celluloid.

"Over-exposed!" rasped Overton. "A hell of a photographer you are!"

"I sure am!" Jim agreed, still gazing ruefully at the ruined negatives. "Funny, though. The camera was checked before I started. I had the range before I pulled the trigger, every shot." He paused, then added, as though reluctant to excuse himself: "It must have been the heat."

"Yeah. I suppose so! Well, that was damn expensive heat for you, my lad. It cost you ten thousand bucks."

"Yes, but—"

Jim had been going to say it had nearly cost him his life but thought better of it. Besides, an idea had come.

"Give me those negatives!" he said, "I'm going to find out what's wrong with 'em."

And since they were of no use to Overton, he gave them to Jim.

THAT night again, Jim Carter presented himself at the Wentworth home in Hartford, and again it was Joan who admitted him.

"Oh, Jimmy!" she murmured, as he took her in his arms. "We're all so proud of you!"

"I'm glad someone is," he said.

"But what a fearful risk you ran! If you hadn't been able to get your motor started—"

"Why think of unpleasant things?" he said with a smile.

Then they went into the library, where Professor Wentworth added his congratulations.

"But I'm afraid I didn't accomplish much," said Jim, explaining about the pictures.

"Let me see them," said the professor.

Jim handed them over.

For a moment or two Professor Wentworth examined them intently, holding them this way and that.

"They indeed appear to be extremely over-exposed," he admitted at length. "Your Fire Ants are doubtless radio-active to a high degree. The results could not have been much worse had you tried to photograph the sun direct."

"I thought as much," said Carter, gloomily.

"But possibly the damage isn't irreparable. Suppose we try re-developing a few of these negatives."

He led the way to his study, which since the destruction of the observatory had been converted into a temporary laboratory.

TEN minutes later, Professor Wentworth had his re-developing bath ready in a porcelain basin and had plunged some of the negatives into it.

"This process is what photographers call intensification," he explained. "It consists chemically in the oxidation of a part of the silver of which the image is composed. I have here in solution uranium nitrate, plus potassium ferricyanide acidified with acetic acid. The latter salt, in the presence of the acid, is an oxidizing agent, and, when applied to the image, produces silver oxide, which with the excess of acetic acid forms silver acetate."

"Which is all so much Greek to me!" said Carter.

"At the same time, the ferricyanide is reduced to ferrocyanide," the professor went on, with a smile at Joan, "whereupon insoluble red uranium ferrocyanide is produced, and, while some of the silver, in being oxidized by this process, is rendered soluble and removed from the negative into the solution, it is replaced by the highly non-actinic and insoluble uranium compound."

The process was one quite familiar to photographers experienced in astronomical work, he explained. In fifteen minutes they should know what results they were getting.

But when fifteen minutes passed and the negatives were still as black as ever, Jim's hope waned.

Not so Professor Wentworth's, however.

"There is a definite but slow reaction taking place," he said after a careful examination. "Either the over-exposure is even greater than I had suspected, or the actinic rays from your interesting subjects have formed a stubborn chemical union with the silver of the image. In the latter event, which is the theory I am going to work on, we must speed up the reaction and tear some of that excess silver off, if we're ever to see what is underneath."

"But how are you going to speed up the reaction?" asked Jim. "I thought that uranium was pretty strong stuff by itself."

"It is, but not as strong as this new substance we have in combination with the silver here. So I think I'll try a little electrolysis—or, in plain English, electro-plating."

As he spoke, the professor clipped a couple of platinum electrodes to the basin, one at each end. To the anode he attached one of the negatives, to the cathode a small piece of iron.

"Now then, we'll soon see."

He passed a low current into the wires, through a rheostat, with startling results. There was a sudden foaming of the solution and a weird vapor rose from it, luminous, milky, faintly orange.

FOR a moment, all they could do was stare.

Then Professor Wentworth switched off the current and stepped toward the tank. Waving away that orange gas, he reached for the cathode and held it up. It was no longer iron, but silver, now.

"Plated, you see!" he exclaimed in triumph.

"Yes, but those fumes!" cried Jim. "Why, they were the same color as the—the Fire Ants, as you call them."

"I know." The professor was not as calm as he pretended. "We have released some of their actinic rays captured by the negative, in prying loose our excess silver. Later I shall repeat the process and capture some of that vapor for analysis. At present, let us have a look at the negative already treated."

He lifted the anode from the solution now, removed the negative, and held it up. A smile of satisfaction broke over his face, followed by a shudder.

"There you are, Jim! Have a look!"

Jim looked, with Joan peering over his shoulder, and his pulses tingled. It was a clear shot of that scattering half-circle of fiery termites, taken after he got away and swept back over them.

"Say, that's wonderful!" he exclaimed.

"Wonderful—but horrible!" echoed Joan.

"I'll admit they're not much on looks," laughed Carter. "But their homely maps are worth a lot to me—ten thousand dollars, in fact!"

He told her why, and what he proposed to do with the money, and Joan thought it a very good idea.

While this was taking place, Professor Wentworth was re-developing the rest of the negatives.

At last all had been salvaged, even those taken in the terrific heat over that weird glass city out there, and Jim was preparing to bear them back to Overton in triumph.

He had thanked the kindly professor from the bottom of his heart, had even told him something of what he had been telling Joan. There remained but to put one last question, then go.

"Summing it all up, what do you make of those nightmares?" he asked. "Do you think they can be destroyed?"

Professor Wentworth did not reply at once.

"I can perhaps answer your question better when I have analyzed this specimen of gas," he said at length, holding up a test-tube in which swirled a quantity of that luminous, milky orange vapor. "But if you wish to quote me for publication, you may say that when I have learned the nature of it, I shall devote all my energies to combating the menace it constitutes."

And that was the message Jim took back with him, but it was the pictures that interested the practical Overton most.

BEFORE many days, however, Overton, with the rest of the world, was turning anxiously to Professor Wentworth, watching his every move, awaiting his every word. For before many days terrible reports started coming in, not only from the Arizona desert but from the assembly grounds of the Fire Ants everywhere.

Those deadly termites were on the move! They were spreading from their central citadels in ominous, expanding circles—circles that engulfed villages, towns and cities in a swift, relentless ring of annihilation that was fairly stupefying.

In North America, the cities of Phoenix, Tucson and Prescott, with all that lay between, were already gone, their frantic populaces fleeing to the four points of the compass before that fateful orange tide. In South America, Rosario and Cordoba were within the flaming ring and Buenos Aires was threatened. In Europe, Moscow and its vast tributary plain had fallen before the invaders. In Asia, a veritable inland empire was theirs, reaching from Urga to the Khingan Mountains. In Africa, Southern Algeria and French Sudan, with their innumerable small villages and oases, were overrun. In Australia, Coolgardie had succumbed and Perth was in a panic.

But fearful though the destruction was on the continents, it was the islands of the world that suffered most. First the smallest, those picturesque green gems of the South Seas, crisped and perished. Then came reports of the doom of the Hawaiian group, the Philippines, the East and West Indies, New Zealand, Tasmania and a score of others, their populations perishing by the thousands, as shipping proved unavailable to transport them to safety.

By far the most tragic fate, however, was that suffered by the British Isles. What happened there stunned the world, and brought realization to humanity that unless some miracle intervened, it was but a mirror of the doom that awaited all. For England, Ireland and Scotland were habitable no more. London, Dublin, Glasgow—all their proud cities, all their peaceful hamlets, centuries old, were flaming ruins.

Out of a population, of some sixty millions, it was estimated that at least eight millions must have perished. The rest, by prodigious feats of transportation, managed to reach the mainland, where they spread as refugees throughout an apprehensive, demoralized Europe.

AS for the armies and navies of the world, they were powerless before this fiendish invader. Hammered with high explosives, drenched with chemicals, sprayed with machine-gun ballets, the fiery termites surged on unchecked, in ever-widening circles of death.

Lead and steel passed through them harmlessly. Gas wafted off them like air. Despite the frantic efforts of scientists and military men, nothing could be devised to stem that all-devouring orange tide.

It was quite obvious by now, even to the most conservative minds, that the end of human life on earth was not far off. It could only be a few more weeks before the last stronghold fell. Daily, hourly, those deadly Fire Ants were everywhere expanding their fields of operations. Presently all humanity would be driven to the seacoasts, there to perish by fire or water, as they chose.

There were some optimists, of course, who believed that the miracle would happen—that Professor Wentworth or some other scientist would devise some means of repelling the invader before it was too late.

Young Jim Carter of *The York Press* was not among them, however, though he would have gambled it would be Professor Wentworth if anyone. For what hope was there that any mere man could figure out a weapon that would be effective against such a deadly, such a superhuman foe?

Very little, it seemed, and he grew less and less sanguine, as he continued his frenzied, sleepless work of reporting the unending catastrophes for his paper.

He often thought bitterly of that ten thousand dollars. A lot of good that would do him now!

As for Joan, she faced her fate with fortitude—fortitude and a supreme faith that her father would succeed in analyzing that sinister orange vapor and find the weapon the world waited for.

But agonizing days passed and he did not find it.

Then at last, on the night of August 14th, when Los Angeles and San Francisco were smoldering infernos, along with Reno, Denver, Omaha, El Paso and a score of other great American cities; when Buenos Aires and Santiago were gone, Berlin and Peking and Cairo; when Australia was all one fiery hell—then it was that Professor Wentworth summoned Jim Carter to Hartford.

HOPING against hope, he hurried over.

Once again, Joan ushered him into the house. She was very pale and did not speak.

At her side stood her father. It was he who spoke.

"Good evening, Jim. You have come promptly."

His voice was strained, his face grave. He had aged greatly in the past few weeks.

"Well I'll admit I clipped along. You've—found something?"

Professor Wentworth smiled wanly.

"Suppose you step into my study and see what I have found."

He led the way toward the little makeshift laboratory that for many days and nights had been the scene of his efforts.

It was littered with strange devices now, strangest of all perhaps a huge glass tube like a cannon, mounted on some sort of swivel base.

Ignoring this for the moment, he turned to a smaller tube set upright on a table at the far end of the room. In it, glowed a sinister orange lump that made the whole tube fluorescent.

"Behold one of your monsters in captivity!" said the professor, again with a wan smile. "In miniature, of course. What I have done is to condense some of that vapor into a solid."

The process, he explained, was similar to that employed by Madame Curie in obtaining metallic radium—electrolyzing a radium chloride solution with mercury as a cathode, then driving off the mercury by heat in a current of hydrogen—only he had used the new element instead of radium.

"Incidentally, I have learned that this new element is far more radioactive than radium and possesses many curious properties. Among them, it decomposes violently in water—particularly salt water—producing harmless hydrogen and chloride compounds. So we have nothing to fear from those seeds that fell in our oceans, lakes and rivers."

"Well, that's something, anyway," said Jim. "But have you found any way to combat the ones that have already hatched?"

"Before I answer that question," Professor Wentworth replied, "I shall let you witness a little demonstration."

He advanced to the cannon-like device at the other end of the room, swung it on its swivel till it was pointing directly at that fluorescent orange tube on the table.

"Watch closely!" he said, throwing a switch.

There was a sudden, whining hum in the air and the nib of the big tube glowed a soft, velvety green. Jim gazed at the scene with rapt attention.

"Don't look at that one!" whispered Joan. "Look at the other!"

Jim did so, and saw that its fluorescence was waning.

A moment more the professor held the current on, while the tube grew white. Then he threw off the switch.

"Now let us have a look at our captive," he said, striding over.

They followed, and one glance told Jim what had happened. That sinister lump of orange metal had vanished.

BUT where was it? That was what he wanted to know.

"A natural question, but not one easy to answer," was Professor Wentworth's reply. "I shall tell you what I have done; then you may judge for yourself."

The cannon-like device which had accompanied the seeming miracle was an adaptation of the cathode tube, whose rays are identical with the beta rays of the atom and consist of a stream of negatively charged particles moving at the velocity of light—186,000 miles a second. These rays, in theory, have the power to combine with the positively charged alpha rays of the atom and drag them from their electrons, causing them to discharge their full quanta of energy at once, in the form of complete disintegration—and it was this theory the professor had acted on.

"But, good Lord—that's splitting the atom!" exclaimed Jim. "You don't mean to say you've done that?"

"I apparently have," was the grave admission. "But do not let it seem such a miracle. Bear in mind, as I have pointed out before, that nature has accomplished this alchemy many times. All radio-active elements are evidences of it. The feat consists merely in altering the valence of the atom, changing its electric charge, in other words. What I have done in the present instance is merely to speed up a process nature already had under way, inasmuch as we are dealing with a radio-active substance."

"But what has happened to the by-product of the reaction?"

"Your guess is as good as mine. I have not had time to study that phase of it. Heat, mainly, was produced. Possibly a few atoms of helium. But the substance is gone. That is our chief concern just now."

It was only after abandoning chemical means and turning to physics that he had met with success, he said. Cathode rays had finally proved the key to the riddle.

"But do you think this thing will work on a big scale?" asked Jim regarding that fragile tube doubtfully.

Professor Wentworth hesitated before replying.

"I do not know," he admitted, "but I intend to find out—to-night."

JIM looked at him in amazement. "To-night?"

"Yes. Or rather, the experiment will be at dawn. If successful, this continent at least will be rid of the menace."

Jim's amazement turned to incredulity and a sudden fear gripped him. Had the strain of the past few weeks unbalanced the professor's mind?

"But surely you can't hope to wipe them out with one tube. Why, it would take hundreds."

"No, only one. You see, I am going to place the tube in the center of the circle and direct its rays outward toward the circumference in a swinging radius."

Whereupon, for a moment, Jim's fear seemed confirmed.

"But, good God!" he exclaimed. "It couldn't possibly be that powerful, could it?"

"I think it can be made to be," was Professor Wentworth's grave assurance. "The greatest power we know in the universe is radiant energy, which reaches us from the sun and the stars, traveling at the speed of light."

"Like light rays, these heat rays can be focused, directed; and the beta rays of the cathode, traveling at the same velocity, can be made to ride these rays of radiant heat much as electric power rides radio waves. The giant, in short, can be made, to carry the dwarf, with his deadly little weapon. That, at least, is the theory I am acting on."

This somewhat allayed Jim's fears—fears that vanished when the professor went on to explain somewhat the working of his mechanism.

"But how are you going to get the thing out there?" he asked, picturing with a shudder the center of the flaming hell.

"I imagine the War Department will provide me with a volunteer plane and pilot for the purpose," was the calm reply.

"And you will go?"

"Yes, I will go."

Jim debated, but not for long.

"Well, you needn't trouble the War Department. Here's your volunteer pilot! The plane's outside. When do we start?"

"But, my dear young man!" objected the professor. "I cannot permit you to make this sacrifice. It is suicide, sheer suicide."

"Is my life any more precious than yours, or that of some volunteer Army pilot?" Jim asked him.

"But there is Joan. If I fail—she must depend on you."

"If you fail, Professor, Joan won't need me or anyone, for long. No, I go. So let's chuck the argument and get ready."

"Oh, Jimmy!" sobbed Joan. "Jimmy!"

But her eyes, as they met his mistily, were lit with a proud splendor.

TWO hours later, Jim Carter's little auto-plane lifted into the night, and, with that precious tube mounted above the cabin, winged swiftly westward.

As on his former foray into that fiery realm, Jimmy timed his flight to arrive over the eastern edge of the Arizona desert just before dawn. Somewhere in that great sandy waste, they felt, there would be a place to set the plane down and get the ray going.

Professor Wentworth had broadcast the particulars of his tube to his scientific colleagues wherever humanity still remained, and the eyes of the world were on this flight. If successful, swift planes would bear similar tubes to the centers of the devastated regions elsewhere, and sweep outward with their deadly rays. The earth would be rid of this fiery invader. If it were not successful....

Jim preferred not to think of that, as he drove on into the night.

Crossing the Missouri River at dark and deserted Kansas City, they soon saw the eastern arc of that deadly orange circle loom on the horizon. To get over it safely, Jim rose to twenty thousand feet, but even there the heat, as they sped across the frontier into enemy territory, was terrific.

Anxiously he watched his revs and prayed for his motor to hold up. If it stopped now, they were cooked!

The sturdy engine purred on with scarcely a flutter, however, and soon they were behind the lines, in a region pitted with the smoldering fires of towns and cities.

It made them shudder, it presented such an appalling panorama of ruin. But at the same time, it strengthened their hope. For very few flares of orange gleamed now among the red. The main forces of the invader were at the front. That meant there should be a safe place to land somewhere.

AN hour later, some miles beyond that weird glass citadel that had been their objective, they found a wide stretch of empty desert, and there Jim brought the little plane down to a faultless landing, just as dawn was lightening the east.

Stepping out, he drew a deep breath of relief. For had he crashed, or smashed that fragile tube, all would have been in vain.

"Well, here we are!" he exclaimed, grimly cheerful, as Professor Wentworth stepped out after him. "Now let's—"

Then he broke off, horrified, as he saw another figure follow the professor from the cabin.

"Joan!" he gasped.

"Present!" she replied.

"But, my daughter!" the professor's voice broke in. "My dear child!" A sob shook him. "Why, why, this is—"

"Please don't let's talk about it!" she begged, giving his arm a little pat. "I'm here and it can't be helped now. I was only afraid you'd find me before it was too late and take me back."

Then, edging over to Jim and slipping her arm in his, she murmured:

"Oh, my dear! Don't you see I couldn't stay behind? I had to be with you at the end, Jimmy, if—"

"It won't be!" he cried, pressing her cold hand. "It can't be!"

Then he turned to give his attention to her father, who had already mounted to the cockpit and was working absorbedly over his mechanism in the pale light of the coming day.

Any moment, Jim knew, those flaming termites might discover them, and come swooping down. With keen eyes he scanned the horizon. No sign of them yet.

"How are you up there?" he called.

"About ready," was the reply. "But I shall want more light than this for my mirrors."

Tensely, counting the seconds, they waited for the sunrise....

AND now, as they waited, suddenly a sinister tinge of orange suffused the rosy hues of the east.

"The Fire Ants!" cried Joan, shrinking. "They've seen us! They're coming!"

It was true, Jim saw with a heavy heart.

Turning to Professor Wentworth, he gasped out:

"Quick! We've got to do something! You've no idea how fast they move!"

"Very well." The professor's voice was strangely calm. "You may start your motor. I shall do what I can. Though if we only had the sun—"

Jim leaped for the cabin.

A touch of the starter and the powerful engine came in. Braking his wheels hard, to hold the plane on the ground, he advanced the throttle as much as he dared, and sent a high-tension current surging through the wires the professor had connected with his tube above.

Soon came that high, whining hum they had heard in the laboratory—a thousand times magnified now—and the nib of the big tube glowed a livid, eery green in the lemon dawn.

"Joan!" called her father sharply. "Get in the cabin with Jim!"

She did so, her eyes still fixed in horrified fascination on the eastern horizon; and in that tense instant, she saw two things. First, a great orange arc of fiery termites, bearing down on them; and second, another arc, far greater—the vast saffron rim of the rising sun.

Those two things Joan saw—and so did Jim—as their eardrums almost burst with the stupendous vibration that came from the gun in the cockpit. Then they saw a third, something that left them mute with awe.

As Professor Wentworth swung his cannon ray upon that advancing horde, it melted, vanished, leaving only the clear yellow of the morning sunlight before their bewildered eyes.

BUT the professor did not cease. For five minutes—ten, fifteen—he swung that mighty ray around, stepping up its power, lengthening its range, as it reached its invisible, annihilating arm farther and farther out....

Meanwhile Jim was radio-phoning frantically. The air seemed strangely full of static.

At last he got Overton of *The New York Press*.

"Carter speaking, out in Arizona," he said. "Getting any reports on the ray?"

And back came the tremendous news:

"Results! Man, the world's crazy! They're gone—everywhere! Tell the professor to lay off, before he sends us scooting too."

"Right!" said Jim, cutting his motor. "More later!"

And to Professor Wentworth he called:

"All right, that's enough! That ray was stronger than you knew!"

But there came no answer, and mounting to the wing-tip, Joan following, Jim saw a sight that froze him with horror. They beheld the professor, slumped against the tube, his whole body glowing a pale, fluorescent green.

"Father!" screamed Joan, rushing to his side. "Oh, Father!"

The man stirred, motioned her away, gasped weakly:

"Do not touch me, child—until the luminosity goes. I am highly radio-active. I had no time to—insulate the tube. No time to find out how. Had to—hurry—"

His voice waned off and they knew he was dead. The two stood there stunned by the realization of his great sacrifice.

He and Joan had set forth on this venture knowing they stood at least a chance, thought Jim, but Professor Wentworth had known from the start that it was sure death for him.

THE sun stood out above the eastern horizon like a huge gold coin, bright with the promise of life to spend, when Jim and Joan took off at last for the return home; but the radiance of the morning was dimmed by the knowledge of the tragic burden they bore.

For some moments, as they winged on, both were silent.

"Look!" said Jim at length. "Look ahead, Joan!"

She looked, brightened somewhat.

"Yes, I see."

And after a moment, lifting her hazel eyes to his, she said. "Oh, Jimmy, I'm sure it means happiness for us."

"Yes, I'm sure!"

She stirred, moved closer.

"Jimmy, you—you're all I have now."

He made no reply, save to press her trembling hand. But it was enough.

Silently, understandingly, they winged onward into the morning light.